This book belongs to

Bennett Dillon

Published by Redemptorist Publications
Wolf's Lane, Chawton, Hampshire, GU34 3HQ, UK
Tel. +44 (0)1420 88222, Fax. +44 (0)1420 88805
Email rp@rpbooks.co.uk, www.rpbooks.co.uk

A registered charity limited by guarantee
Registered in England 3261721

Edited by Rachel Thompson
Illustrated and Designed by Emma Repetti

ISBN 978-0-85231-527-9

Printed by GPS Colour Graphics Ltd, Belfast.

For our four very special grandchildren:
Liam, Kieran, Alexander and Olivia

The Animals' CHRISTMAS

Aileen Urquhart

Illustrated by Emma Repetti

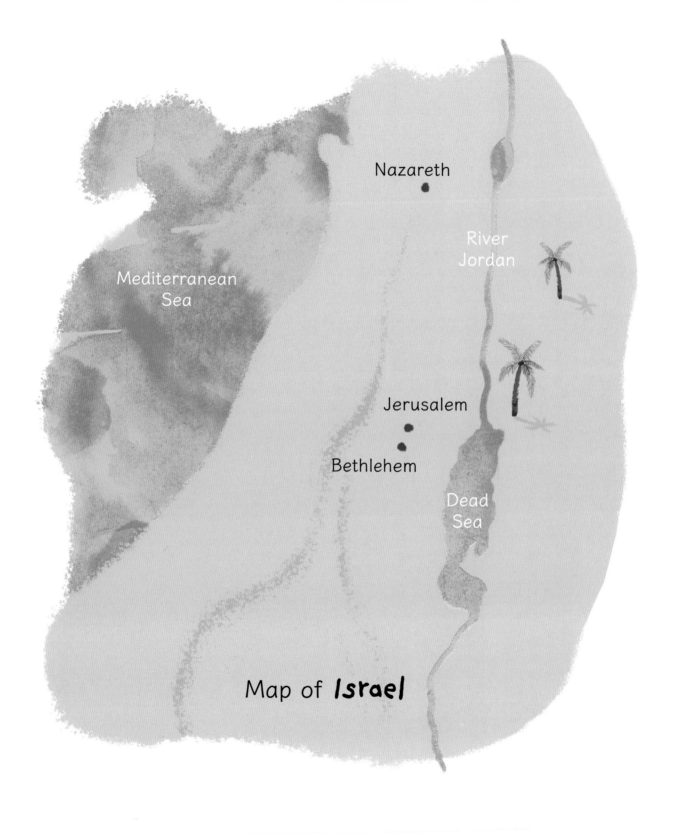

Nazareth

River
Jordan

Mediterranean
Sea

Jerusalem

Bethlehem

Dead
Sea

Map of **Israel**

Contents

Mary's house in **Nazareth**

Sarah the Spider

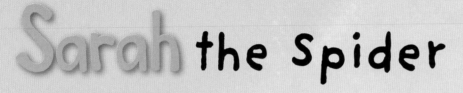

Hello, I'm Sarah the Spider. I live in the best house in Nazareth. It isn't the biggest house. It isn't the fanciest house. It's the house where Mary lives with her mum and dad.

Mary helps with the mending and baking and cleaning. She is good at these things, but her mum and dad don't think she is good at cleaning. That's because she **never, never, NEVER** sweeps away my web. Mary knows I need a web to catch my food, and she knows I will keep the house free from flies. And that is why I live in the best house in Nazareth.

3

One day Mary was sitting down quietly, mending a hole in her cloak, when there was a sudden **brightness shining** all around. It wasn't from the sun. It was an angel. And guess what? This beautiful angel, **all shimmering with joy**, knelt down at Mary's feet and kissed them.

4

"Hail, Mary, full of grace!" the angel said.

And then he gave Mary a very important message. I know it was important, because an angel wouldn't normally come from heaven with an ordinary message. The angel told Mary she was to have a **baby** who would **save the world**.

5

I didn't understand this. Neither did Mary, and she asked how it would happen. When the angel said to trust in God, she agreed.

I didn't realise that I would never see Mary's baby. I thought Mary would stay here with her mum and dad, or go down the road and live with Joseph. But Mary and Joseph went away on Daniel the Donkey and I never saw them again.

This was sad for me,
but I went on to have
hundreds of spiderlings,
I told them the story, and
somehow I knew that the
world was a beautiful
place where angels give
messages of **hope** and
that **God is with us all**.
So I was also full of **joy**.

Daniel the Donkey

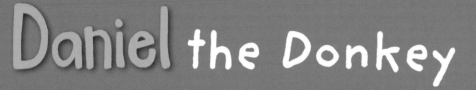

Hi, I'm Daniel the Donkey. I am six years old, which is quite grown up for a donkey. I am Joseph's donkey and I am glad about that.

Joseph is a **kind master**. He always makes sure I have plenty of water to drink.

Most of the time I work for Joseph around the town of
Nazareth. He makes things from wood, like door frames and
yokes for the oxen, so I have to carry the wood to his workshop.
He never makes me carry too much. Sometimes he lets the
children of Nazareth ride on my back. This is **fun**. Usually.

One day, Joseph untied me from my tree and loaded some food and clothes on my back. Then we set off for Mary's house, and she added some more stuff. It wasn't too heavy.

We walked a **long, long way**. Further than I have ever walked in my life. At first I was happy. Mary was **singing** a little, and Joseph began **whistling**. We passed through villages and towns as we made our way south. We saw other people walking along too. Where were they all going?

After four days I was cross and tired. Mary
was tired too and sometimes she would sit on
my back while Joseph carried their bundles.

At last we reached a place called Bethlehem. Joseph
tried lots of inns to find a place for them to sleep, but
the town was so busy. **Everywhere was full**.

Eventually someone let them **sleep in a
stable**. This suited me very well. It was
dry and warm, and a kind ox let me share
his food. Well, he did have a lot there.

13

Obadiah the Ox

I'm Obadiah the Ox.
You can call me Ob
for short. I wasn't
too pleased when a
donkey turned up to
share my stable.

I stood quite still, and wouldn't move out of the way for him in case he wanted my hay. But then I noticed the two people.

Joseph was so kind to Mary. He looked **very, very tired**, but he got busy making a bed of straw for Mary. She looked even more tired, and I could see she was going to **have a baby** very soon.

15

I felt ashamed of being mean about my food, so I budged up a bit for Daniel the Donkey. There was plenty for us both really.

16

It was so **peaceful** in the stable, even though it now had a man, a woman and a donkey in it as well as me. Daniel the Donkey fell asleep, and then so did I. But I don't think Mary and Joseph slept, because when I woke up there was **somebody else there**.

A **tiny baby** was snuggled up in Mary's lap. They called him Jesus. And what do you think Mary did then? She took the baby and laid him in the manger. Right where my food was. And I didn't even feel cross. He was such a **little beauty**.

I'll let Lilah the Lamb tell you some more of the story, as she came here specially when an **angel** gave her a message.

Lilah the Lamb

Hello, I'm Lilah. The angel didn't really give me the message. I just said that to Ob to show off. Here is the real story. I was cuddling in to my mum with my twin, Laban. I'm two minutes older than he is, so I'm **bigger** and **braver**. But I was suddenly very frightened. I'm not ashamed to say this, as my mum was frightened too, and so were the shepherds.

The reason is... there was a sudden **blazing glory** in the sky, and the whole world was filled with beautiful singing.

Then an angel
appeared,
and told me –
I mean told the
shepherds –
not to be afraid.
The angel said
an **amazing** thing
had happened.
A baby had been
born. Well, babies are
being born all the time,
and they are all special.

Just look at me and Laban. But
this one was extra special. He was
the **SAVIOUR OF THE WORLD**.
He was bringing peace and
goodwill to us all.

The shepherds hurried down the hill to find the baby Jesus, who would be in a manger, and they brought me with them. And I thoughtfully asked if Laban could come as well, as he looked a bit sad. So Laban knows my story is true. We found the baby, sleeping in the hay.

I knew he was **special**, because the angel said so, and because everything seemed **special** that night, even though it was also very ordinary. But then some more visitors came, and their story was extraordinary. Khalid the Camel wants to tell you all about it, and I am letting him, as I wasn't even born when his story starts.

Khalid the Camel

Greetings! I'm Khalid the Camel. My part of the story started weeks ago, when my master and his two friends got very excited about a **star** in the sky. They said it meant a king had been born, and they had to follow it or they would regret it for the rest of their lives.

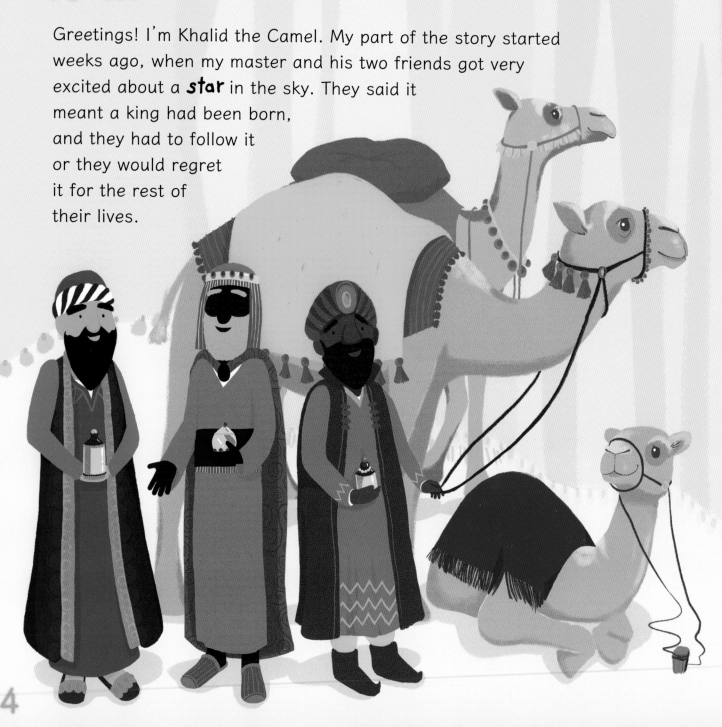

So the three men wisely packed food and clothes for the journey, and loaded up me and my friends, Kanika and Kek. Then they jumped up on to our backs, and the journey began. It took a **long, long time**, as we could only travel by night, when the star was shining brightly.

At last, they came to a busy little town, and the star shone down brightly on a stable. We all crowded in, and it really was a crowd. As well as three **wise** men, three **wise** camels, two **playful** lambs, three **poor** shepherds, one **strong** ox, one **placid** donkey, a **kind** looking man, and a **happy** looking woman, there, right in the middle, lying in a manger, was a **tiny** baby.

Our masters, in all their finery, got down on their knees in the dusty straw, and gave the baby three presents – **gold**, **frankincense** and **myrrh**. Everyone looked very pleased.

27

This is the end of my story. But it isn't the end of the Jesus' story. My wise master had given him gold, because the baby was a **king**. Kanika's master had given him frankincense, because the baby was **holy**. Kek's master had given the baby myrrh, because he would have **sadness** as well as **happiness** in his life. I knew all this because I wisely listened to the men talking.

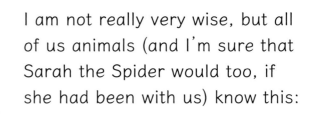

I am not really very wise, but all of us animals (and I'm sure that Sarah the Spider would too, if she had been with us) know this:

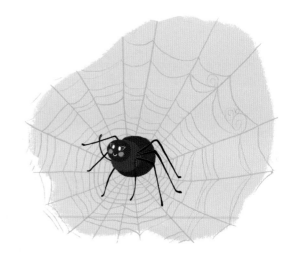

This story is about the most wonderful baby in the whole wide world, and all babies, whoever they are and wherever they are born, share his beauty and his glory, for ever and ever.

29